Wednesday dedicates this book
to the neighborhood.

Copyright © 2016 Philip C. Stead
A Neal Porter Book
Published by Roaring Brook Press
Roaring Brook Press is a division of Holtzbrinck Publishing Holdings Limited Partnership
175 Fifth Avenue, New York, New York 10010
The artwork for this book was handmade using monoprint techniques and collage. All photographs were taken
with a Polaroid 300 Instant Camera. The text was typed by the author on a Smith-Corona Secretarial typewriter.
mackids.com

Library of Congress Cataloging-in-Publication Data

Stead, Philip Christian, author, illustrator.
    Ideas are all around / Philip C. Stead. — First edition.
        pages cm
    "A Neal Porter Book."
    Summary: In search of writing ideas, an author takes a walk with his
dog around the neighborhood.
    ISBN 978-1-62672-181-4 (hardback)
    [1. Authors—Fiction. 2. Authorship—Fiction. 3. Neighborhoods—Fiction.] I. Title.

PZ7.S808566Id 2016
[E]—dc23
                                                                    2015013183

Our books may be purchased in bulk for promotional, educational, or business use. Please
contact your local bookseller or the Macmillan Corporate and Premium Sales Department
at (800) 221-7945 ext. 5442 or by e-mail at MacmillanSpecialMarkets@macmillan.com

First edition 2016
Book design by Philip C. Stead
Printed in China by RR Donnelley Asia Printing Solutions Ltd., Dongguan City, Guangdong Province
1 3 5 7 9 10 8 6 4 2

Ideas Are All Around

PHILIP C. STEAD

A NEAL PORTER BOOK
ROARING BROOK PRESS
NEW YORK

Today
outside my house
the sunflower opened up.

"Hello, Sunflower!"

I planted it from a packet
of very old seeds.

There were a lot of seeds
but only this one grew.

Actually there was one more.

But it fell down in a rainstorm
before it could open.

Planting a seed is always a risk.

*   *   *

I have to write a story today.

That is my job. I write stories.
But today I don't have any ideas.

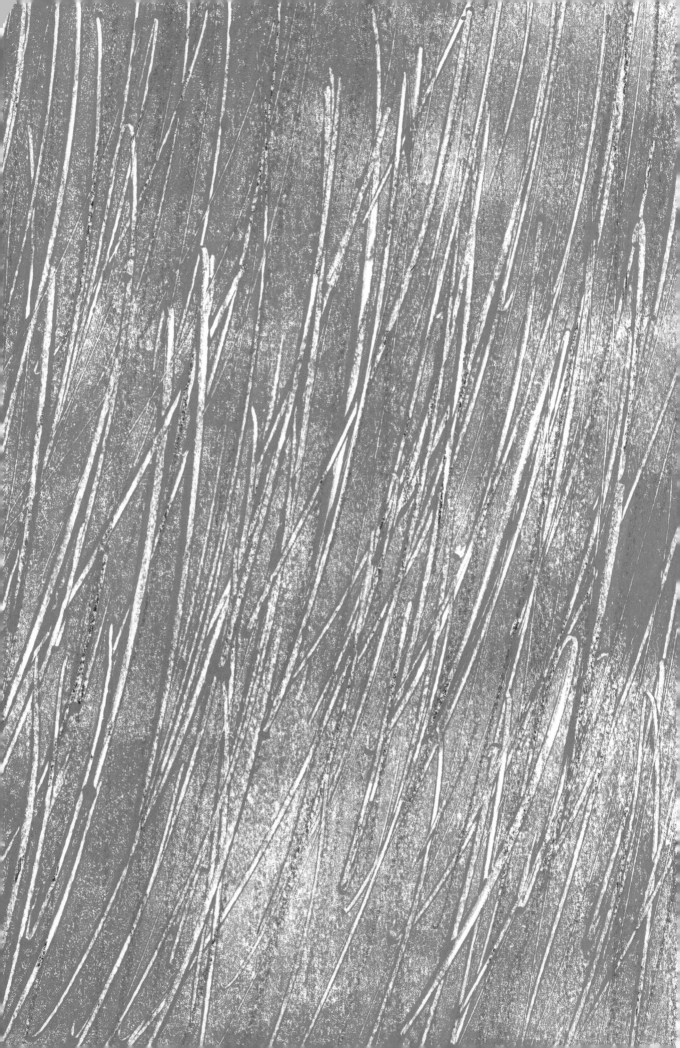

This is my dog, Wednesday.

She doesn't like me to write stories.
It's sunny out
and Wednesday wants to go for a walk.

"C'mon, Wednesday, let's go."

Together we walk over the bridge
down the concrete stairs
then under the bridge
and across the boardwalk
beside the river rolling lazily by.

There
on a small log
is a painted turtle
sitting very still
in a pocket of sunshine.

His name is Frank.

"Hello, Frank!" I say.
And like each time before
he makes quick for the dark water
and disappears.

"Goodbye, Frank."

Someday
I hope he looks forward
to these smidgeons of time we share.

Me and Frank
we're in this together after all.

"H-i-i-i-i, Wednesday!" comes a loud voice
all the way from up the hill
on the other side of the river.

It's Barbara.
Wednesday loves Barbara.

Barbara lives in the back
of a tall blue house
with two dogs
three cats
and an aquarium full of tropical fish.

I used to live in the blue house, too
in a room at the very top.

One day
I tripped on the front steps
carrying a bucket of blue paint.
The bucket flew out of my hands
and the paint made
a big blue blob on the sidewalk.

When Barbara came home she said,
"HOW WONDERFUL...

"A BLUE HORSE!"

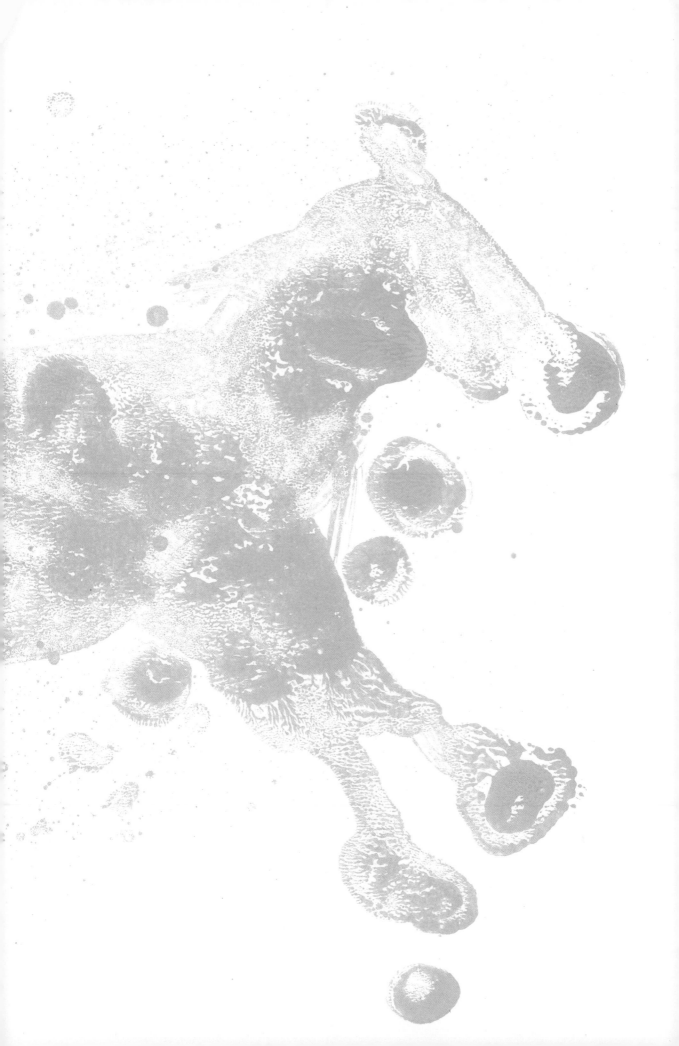

"H-e-y-y-y-y, Barbara!" I call out.
"Maybe we'll stop by later!"

"Okay!" she says. "I'll make coffee!"

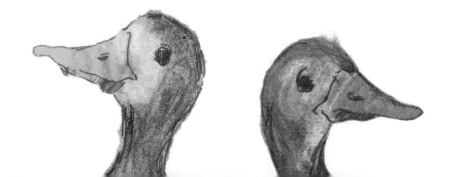

Then comes a line of ducks
floating downstream.

"Hello," I say.
"I don't have any ideas today."

If the ducks have any advice
they keep it to themselves.

Written in spray paint
on the boardwalk near my feet
are the words

STOP WAR

which is a pretty good idea
if you ask me.

"What do you think?" I ask
a tall bird standing in the water.

The bird flies away
when Wednesday gets too close.

HOW WONDERFUL!

TWEET-tweet

Up ahead
a train rumbles by.

I wave
and imagine passengers
off to places like

CHICAGO

OMAHA

SEATTLE

DING!
DING! DING!
DING!

"You should never
walk on train tracks,"
I say to Wednesday.

But we do it anyway.

If we follow them far enough
we'll end up in

CLEVELAND

BALTIMORE

NEW YORK CITY

But instead
we walk uphill
past the school
and around the big purple house.

We stop at the stone church
where a long line of people are waiting
for the soup kitchen.

"Nice day for a walk,"
a woman says to Wednesday.

A man in a wheelchair bends down
and scratches Wednesday behind the ears.
"I used to have a dog just like you!"
he says.

Wednesday wags her tail
and more people come to say hello.

No one seems to notice me.

So I wait
and watch the blue sky.

                    *   *   *

Maybe I'll use my typewriter today.
A typewriter makes writing fun
even when there's nothing to say.
CLAK-CLAK-CLAK, you take a walk on the page.

I bought my typewriter
from a man with thick glasses.

"Hello!" he said. "Come on in!"
"Did you fix all of these?" I asked.
"Fix and repair, that's what I do."
"Do you have a favorite one?"

He looked all around.

"You know, I really don't.
It's like when a person loves horses.
Each one has a different personality.
I love them all."

                    *   *   *

Wednesday tugs the leash
so we start to walk again.

There are a lot of birds out today.
I can hear them
but I'm not good at seeing them.

I have to imagine what they look like.

LEE-dee-WEEP

chik-chik-chik

POH-weet

I know one real birdcall.
The black-capped chickadee goes:
TWEET-tweet. High then low.

It is the same sound I make
when Wednesday chases a squirrel
and I want her to come back...

TWEET-tweet!

"Wednesday!" says Barbara.
"It's so good to see you!"

I come following after.
"Hi, Barbara. How's it going?"

"Pretty good," she says.
"How are things?"

"I have to write a story today."

"Wonderful!"

"But I don't have any ideas."

"Oh," says Barbara,
"I wouldn't worry about it.
Ideas are all around."

We sit on the front steps
and drink coffee together.

Wednesday watches for squirrels.

Barbara tells me about the skunk
that's been living in her cellar lately.

"We keep each other company," she says.

Barbara tells me
about the canoe she'd like to buy.

"There are so many things
you never get to see
if you don't get out on the water."

I tell Barbara about Frank.

We talk about typewriters
and the birdcalls we know.

We talk about long lines of people
waiting for something to eat.

We talk about places
we'd like to go on the train.

We talk about war.

"It's such a waste," Barbara says.
"We could all go fishing instead."

Then Barbara gets up
and pulls a weed from the front yard.

"Did you know
that ten thousand years ago
this spot was the bottom of a lake?

"It's true!
Giant ancient fish
swam in herds
like buffalo.

And before that
were the woolly mammoths."

This neighborhood has seen so many things.

"Let's go," I say.
And they follow me home
like friendly ghosts.

CLAK-CLAK-CLAK
CLAK-CLAK-DING!

Together
we take a walk on the page.

Wednesday falls asleep
and dreams of squirrels.